Peppa Pig™

Cold Winter Day

It is a cold winter day. Peppa and George
have wrapped up warm in their hats, scarves
and mittens to go and feed the ducks.

"Look – it's a muddy puddle," cries Peppa.
Peppa loves jumping in muddy puddles.

She runs over to the puddle but,
as she tries to jump in, she slips!

"Oh! It's frozen solid!" she says.

"Hee! Hee!" snorts George.
"It's not funny, George," says Peppa.

Daddy Pig loves muddy puddles, too!
"Be careful, Daddy!" shouts Peppa.
Daddy Pig has jumped straight
on to the frozen puddle.

"Whoa!" says Daddy Pig, wobbling about. "It's lucky I'm so good at balancing."

Muddy puddles are not fun
when they are frozen.

Everyone keeps walking until they find the
duck pond. Peppa and George throw some
bread to the ducks, but it just bounces along
the surface.
The pond is frozen, too!

Peppa and George both giggle as the ducks slide around.
"Sorry for laughing, Mrs Duck," says Peppa.
"But you do look funny!"

"Look! It's snowing," says Daddy Pig.

"I'm going to catch lots of snowflakes!"
shouts Peppa.

"Snort! Snort!" says George, as he tries
to catch them, too.

"Hello, Peppa and George," says Suzy Sheep.
"We're going to have a toboggan race!"
"Please can we go and watch?"
asks Peppa.

"Of course," says Mummy Pig.
"Let's walk up the hill to the start."

Daddy Pig picks up George
because it is too slippery for him
to walk up the hill on his own.
"What about me?" says Peppa.
"It's a bit slippery for me, too."
"Come on, then," says Daddy Pig,
scooping up Peppa.

Mummy Pig tells Daddy Pig to be
extra careful not to fall over.
"Don't worry, Mummy Pig," he says.
"I'm very good at balancing."

At the top of the hill, all the toboggans are just setting off when Daddy Pig topples over and starts skidding down the hill!
He zooms past Danny Dog, Zoe Zebra and Pedro Pony. Soon Daddy Pig is in the lead!

Wheeee!

Peppa and George are
sitting on Daddy Pig's
tummy. "Wheeee!"
they call.
They are enjoying
the ride!

Peppa and George win the race!
"My daddy makes a great toboggan," Peppa tells
everyone. All the children are laughing about
Peppa and George's special toboggan ride.
"It's not funny," says Daddy Pig.

Hee! Hee!

Hee! Hee!

"It is a *bit* funny," says Mummy Pig.
"I suppose it is a *bit* funny," Daddy Pig agrees.
"Hee! Hee! Hee!" everyone laughs.